For Harry Schroeder, a chief in his own right.—B.G.

To all our children —R.R.

Copyright © 1992 Rabbit Ears Productions, Inc., Rowayton, Connecticut.
Rabbit Ears Books is an imprint of Rabbit Ears Productions.
Published by Picture Book Studio, Saxonville, Massachusetts.
Distributed in the United States by Simon & Schuster, New York, New York.
Distributed in Canada by Vanwell Publishing, St. Catharines, Ontario.
All rights reserved.
Printed in Hong Kong.
10 9 8 7 6 5 4 3 2 1

Library of Congress Cataloging-in-Publication Data
Gleeson, Brian.
Koi and the kola nuts / written by Brian Gleeson ; illustrated by Reynold Ruffins.
p. cm.
Summary: Cheated of his rightful inheritance, a chief's son uses a bunch of kola nuts to gain a happy new life.
ISBN 0-88708-281-5 : $14.95
[1. Folklore—Africa.] I. Ruffins, Reynold, ill. II. Title.
PZ8.1.G4594Ko   1992
398.2—dc20
[E]   92-7094
CIP
AC

Koi and the Kola Nuts

Written by Brian Gleeson · Illustrated by Reynold Ruffins

Rabbit Ears Books

ome. Sit down. I will tell you a story that comes from Africa.  It is dawn in the west of Africa. The sun is a big orange-red ball, slowly rising over the horizon. Feel the warm breeze that blows. ⌂ The rains have just come and the earth is full of promise. Flowers bloom, the banana trees bear fruit and the yams and rice grow well in the fields. Smell the beautiful fragrances. ⌂ Look. The animals gather at the river. ⌂ Far in the distance there is a village. The smoke from the cooking fires makes a trail in the sky. ⌂ Listen. You can hear the sound of the drums. The drums spread the news that the chief of a village has died.

🏠 All the people and all the animals from miles around hear the message of the drums: Chief Sadaka is dead.

A palaver—that's a meeting—is called and all the elders of the village gather to decide what to do. They decide that the wisest man of the village will divide the chief's possessions among the sons. So the wise man counts out to each of the sons so many goats, so many cows, so many tusks of ivory, and so many pieces of gold. 🖐 The wise man finishes. But here comes Koi, the chief's youngest son. He's been hunting and no one fetched him when the wise man divided his father's possessions. 🖐 There is nothing left for Koi, not even a tiny chicken bone. 🖐 Since this wise man is wisest when it comes to avoiding work, he does not bother to redivide the chief's possessions. No, no; it is too much work. The wise man looks around and he sees a small, sickly kola tree. 🖐 "Ah, Koi," says the wise man. "And for you we have the kola tree over there." 🖐 "What you say, man?" cries Koi. "My father the chief dies and you give me only this kola tree?" 🖐 Koi is a proud young man. He grows angry, very angry. He cannot abide the slight of the wise man. 🖐 "I will go to a land where I am treated like the son of a chief." 🖐 Koi picks all the kola nuts from the tree and wraps them in a mat. He ties the mat into a kinja, swings the load onto his back and leaves the village. 🖐 "I will never return here," Koi tells the people of his village. "You do not know how to treat the son of a chief!"

Koi walks for nine days with the kinja on his back. The kinja is a heavy load, but the jungle makes good music for him to walk by. The birds sing and the chimpanzees play hide-and-seek amid the elephant grass. Koi watches the zebras galloping across the veld. He walks gently past a sleeping lion and lioness, careful not to awaken them. ✦ Koi comes to the foot of a mountain. It is a big mountain, with the peak hidden by clouds. He climbs the mountain with great difficulty, the kinja getting heavier with each step. Finally, he arrives at the top. He sees the lush valley beneath him. There is a wide, silvery river curling through the valley. ✦ "This will be a good place," says Koi. "Perhaps the people there will know how to treat the son of a chief." ✦ Koi makes his way down the slope. He sees a large snake, but the snake does not see Koi. The snake looks left. The snake looks right. And then he slithers along. "What are you looking for, Friend Snake?" says Koi. ✦ "Oh, it's terrible!" says the snake. "My mother is ill and she needs

kola medicine. I must find some kola nuts to make the medicine that will make her well."

"Look no further," says Koi, as he takes the kinja from his back. "I have kola nuts you may have. Take them. Make the medicine that will make your mother well again." "Oh, you've saved my mother's life," says the snake. "Thank you so very much." "It is nothing," says Koi. "Go quickly now! Your mother now needs the kola medicine."

Koi walks down the mountain, happy that he can help Friend Snake. Koi sees an army of ants marching in an endless column as wide as a zebra's stripe. Koi steps aside to let the ants pass.

As the column passes he hears a tiny, high-pitched voice. "Do you know where we can find a kola tree?" asks the leader of the ants.

"We made a most unfortunate mistake. We ate the Forest Devil's kola nuts. A whole basket full! We must replace them or else the Forest Devil will trample us with his gigantic feet." "How many do you need?" asks Koi.

"He says he wants as many kola nuts as he has fingers and toes. Let's see, I have six feet, and four toes on each foot…" "The Forest Devil is a person," says Koi. "He has ten fingers and ten toes. You need twenty kola nuts."

Koi takes twenty kola nuts from his kinja and gives them to the ants. They put the nuts on their heads and march down the mountain to give the Forest Devil his tribute.

Koi resumes his journey. At the base of the mountain he encounters an alligator. The alligator crawls so very slowly. The alligator is crying. ✻ "What is your trouble?" says Koi. ✻ "I accidently ate the Rain Maker's dog," says the alligator. "I am doomed....If only I had known it was the Rain Maker's dog." ✻ "What difference does it make?" says Koi. "To eat any dog is bad enough, I say." ✻ "What difference does it make?! The difference is that the Rain Maker says he will strike me dead with a lightning bolt, unless I deliver to him a kinja full of kola nuts by sunrise. And there are no kola nuts on this side of the mountain. It will take me two days to find the kola nuts." ✻ "How do you know there are no kola nuts on this side of the mountain?"

says Koi. ✻ Koi unwraps a corner of his mat to show the alligator his kinja full of kola nuts. ✻ "Why, you have many kola nuts," says the alligator. ✻ "Yes, and I will give you the entire kinja full. You need them more than I." ✻ So Koi fastens the kinja to the alligator's back, and the beast hurries to pay his debt to the Rain Maker.

That evening Koi reaches a village. The guard asks: "Who comes to the village of the Great Chief Fulikolli?"  Koi stands proudly and answers: "I am Koi, from the land beyond the mountain. I am the son of Chief Sadaka."  Now Koi is covered with dust and his legs are scratched from the rocks on the mountain. He does not look like a chief's son.  "I have run away from my home because the people there don't know how to treat the son of a chief," says Koi. "May I be the guest of your village?"  "Son of a chief?" says the guard. "You look more like the son of a hyena."  As Koi speaks to the guard, many people from the village gather to see the visitor.  "He's very dusty," says one old woman. "He's no son of a chief. He's just an *osu*, nothing but an outcast."  "Yes, he's just an *osu*," says her husband. "And he'll bring us bad luck, too."  "Send him away," says another man.  "Let's eat him," says a very large and fat woman.  "Let's bury him in the anthill," says a tall man.  "No, let's feed him to the crocodiles," says another man.  "I say cook him in the pot," replies the very large and very fat woman.

The villagers like the fat woman's suggestion. They seize Koi and take him away to the pot. And they chant: *"He's no son of a chief! He's merely a thief! There's nothing worse than an osu with a curse! Let's have a big feast—or a little one at least!"* Koi's body shakes with fear. "Surely, this village does not know how to treat the son of a chief," he says. And a man dressed in a leopard robe emerges from a hut. It is the Great Chief Fulikolli. "What do we have here?" asks Chief Fulikolli. "I am Koi, the son of Chief Sadaka from over the mountain," says Koi. "I ask if I may be a guest of your village, and your people take me to the pot to cook me."

The very large and very fat woman shouts: "He's no son of a chief. He's an *osu*. Let's cook him!"

The villagers agree. They chant: *"He's no son of a chief! He's merely a thief! There's nothing worse than an osu with a curse! Let's have a big feast—or a little one at least!"*

"Wait!" says Chief Fulikolli. "We shall test him first to see if he is truly the son of a chief." 🌴 Koi breathes a sigh of relief. 🌴 Chief Fulikolli speaks: "If the boy chops down that palm tree so that it falls toward the forest—instead of toward the village—we let him go. If the palm falls toward the village...we cook him!" 🌴 The chief's people laugh. The palm leans so sharply toward the village it looks as though the slightest wind will topple it. 🌴 Koi shudders and sweats. This test is impossible. He must think. 🌴 "Please, Chief Fulikolli," he says. "Send your people away and let me cut down the tree after dark." 🌴 "Yes," says Chief Fulikolli. "It is agreed. You have until morning to fell the tree." 🌴 The chief gives Koi an ax, and the villagers go to their huts dreaming of tomorrow's feast.

oi sits beneath the palm to await the night. As he waits, he weeps. He does not know how he will make the palm fall toward the forest. The cooking pot awaits him, he knows. ✲ Koi hears the rustling of leaves and vines. ✲ "Who is it? Speak!" ✲ "It is me, Friend Snake," says a voice in the night. ✲ "I am tracking you all day. I wish to thank you again for the kola nuts you gave to me. My mother is well and she sends you her thanks." ✲ "That is kind of your mother," says Koi. "But my fortune has changed since last we met." ✲ "Is that why you weep?" says Friend Snake. "Tell me." ✲ "I must chop down this palm tree so that it falls toward the forest," says Koi, "or else I shall be cooked." ✲ "But look how it leans. The people of this village must drink too much palm wine!" says Friend Snake. ✲ "Exactly," says Koi. "It's a trick." ✲ "Imagine that," says Friend Snake. "We must play a trick on them. I will get my six uncles, the pythons." ✲ The pythons are Africa's biggest and mightiest snakes. At moonrise Friend Snake returns with his six uncles, the pythons. The great snakes wrap their tails around the leaning palm tree and wrap their necks around a nearby bombax tree. ✲ Koi chops the palm with all his strength. And when the last fiber of the palm is cut, the six uncles pull the tree over so that it falls toward the forest.

hief Fulikolli wakes up the next morning and his people follow him to see whether Koi has passed the test. Koi sits on the felled tree, drinking the milk of a coconut. The tree is in the forest. 🏠 "Look!" says Chief Fulikolli. "The boy shall go free!" 🏠 "It is magic," says a villager. "The boy used *ju-ju* to push the tree into the forest." 🏠 "Cook him in the pot," says the very large and very fat woman. "Let's cook him tonight!" 🏠 The people chant: *"There's nothing worse than an osu with a curse! Let's have a big feast—or a little one at least!"* 🏠 "Quiet!" says Chief Fulikolli. "We will test the boy once more!" 🏠 "We will scatter ten baskets of rice in my fields," says the chief. "If he picks up every grain in the dark of the night he is truly the son of a chief, and I will free him. If he fails, we cook him tomorrow night."

When darkness comes Koi goes out to the fields with a basket. On his hands and knees he feels the ground for the grains of rice. He tries and tries but he can see nothing. It is an impossible task. 🌱 Koi feels hopeless. 🌱 "This is no way to treat the son of a chief," he says. 🌱 A tear rolls down his cheek and falls to the ground. The tear lands on the head of an ant. 🌱 A reedy, high-pitched voice exclaims: "RAIN! ...RAIN!...RAIN! Everybody take cover, the floods have come!" 🌱 "Wait!" says the ant. "Rain isn't salty. Look, it is a boy who is crying. Aren't you the boy who gave us the kola nuts two days ago?" 🌱 "Yes," says Koi. "But now I am in danger. I must gather the ten baskets of rice spread in the fields by morning, or else I shall be cooked." 🌱 "Do not worry, my friend. You bring the baskets and my people will pick up the rice." 🌱 Soon the fields crawl with millions of ants, and each ant carries a grain of rice.

he next morning the ten baskets of rice sit before the hut of Chief Fulikolli. Koi sits in front of the baskets, eating a wild plum. ✶ "You perform well," says the chief. "Now you go free." ✶ The people of the village surround Koi and Chief Fulikolli. ✶ "He is a sorcerer," says one villager. ✶ "He is the devil," says another.

"Whatever he is, he cheats us of a feast," says still another.  "Let Chief Fulikolli free him," whispers the very large and very fat woman to the very short man. "We will catch him outside the village and cook him ourselves." Koi hears what the fat woman says. He speaks to the chief:

"I am afraid to go. Your people want to eat me and they will overtake me when I am outside the village."

hief Fulikolli stands before his people and announces in a big voice: "There will be no feast...yet. I will test the boy one more time. I shall throw my medicine ring into the deepest part of the river. If he brings it back to me, will you honor him as the son of a chief?"

 The people of this village are pleased. In one voice they chant: *"We promise, Chief Fulikolli! We promise, we promise!"*  The chief raises his arms over his head. There is silence.  "It is decided," says the chief.

hief Fulikolli and his people go to the river. The chief throws his medicine ring into the deepest part. Then all go back to the village, leaving Koi alone on the bank. ❦ Koi looks at the deep, dark waters of the river. ❦ "Even Chief Fulikolli tries to destroy me," says Koi. "I do not even swim." Koi wades into the river. He sees the long, gray nose of an alligator gliding toward him. Koi is frightened. The alligator grins when he sees Koi. ❦ "Do you remember me?" asks the alligator. ❦ "I am not so sure," says Koi. "All alligators look the same to me." ❦ "You gave me your kinja full of kola nuts and saved me from the wrath of the Rain Maker," says the alligator. ❦ "I am glad that you still live," says Koi. "As for me, this is the night before I die. I must bring up the chief's

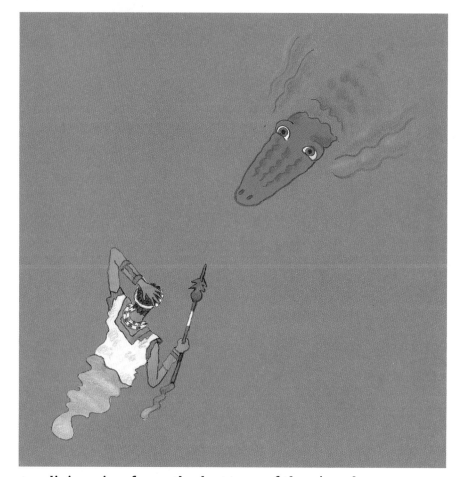

medicine ring from the bottom of the river by dawn, or I shall be cooked." ❦ "You don't say. Perhaps I can help you. I think I swim a little better than you."

he alligator dives under the water and comes up with a small clam shell. He dives again and brings up a fish. The alligator dives in and out and in and out of the water all night.

When the sun begins to rise the alligator comes up for the last time. He has nothing. It is too late. Chief Fulikolli and his people will arrive in moments. Koi is certain he will be cooked.

"I thank you, alligator. You have helped me as though you were my brother. But it is no use. I will be cooked."

hen the alligator smiles. Looped on one of his biggest and sharpest teeth is Chief Fulikolli's medicine ring. 🏠 "That is it!" shouts Koi. "That is it!" 🏠 Koi takes the ring and dances with it to the village. 🏠 When Chief Fulikolli sees that Koi holds the medicine ring he smiles. He takes off his leopard skin robe and puts it on Koi's shoulders. The chief stands before his people and says: "Surely this is the son of a chief!" 🏠 Then the chief claps his hands and the most beautiful woman Koi has ever seen walks out of a nearby hut. 🏠 "And this is my daughter. She shall be your wife." 🏠 Koi turns to Chief Fulikolli and says, "I have found a village where the people know how to treat the son of a chief." 🏠 Suddenly a smile comes over the face of the very large and very fat woman, and she sings: *"We will have a wedding! We will have a wedding tonight! Now we will have a feast! Finally, we will have a feast!"* 🏠 And now the story is over.